SCOOBY-DOO! AND THE SINISTER SORCERER

Written by
James Gelsey

A
LITTLE APPLE
PAPERBACK

SCHOLASTIC INC.

New York Toronto London Auckland Sydney
Mexico City New Delhi Hong Kong Buenos Aires

For Max

ISBN 0-439-42074-1

Designed by Carisa Swenson

12 11 10 9 8 7 6 5 4 3 2 1   3 4 5 6 7 8/0

Special thanks to Duendes del Sur for cover and interior illustrations.
Printed in the U.S.A.
First printing, September 2003

Chapter 1

The Mystery Machine cruised down the highway. As Daphne yawned and stretched her arms out over her head, a soccer ball sailed between them. It ricocheted off the windshield into Velma's lap, then onto the floor.

"SCORE!" Shaggy cried from the back of the van. "Nice shot, Scooby."

"Ranks!" Scooby barked.

"Shaggy! Scooby!" Velma said. "How many times have we told you not to play ball in the van?"

Shaggy and Scooby looked at each other and shrugged.

"Like, I give up," Shaggy said. "How many?"

"We know you're excited about going to the soccer match," Daphne said. "But you really have to be more careful."

"All right, Daphne," Shaggy said. "We're sorry. But you have to admit, it was a pretty good shot."

Shaggy took the ball from Velma and went into the back of the van with Scooby.

"Hey, Scooby, can you do this?" asked Shaggy. He gave the soccer ball a big spin and then tried to balance it on the tip of his finger. The van hit a bump, sending the ball flying into Shaggy's forehead.

"Hey! Watch it, Fred!" Shaggy called.

The van slowed down, then came to a stop.

"Like, what's going on?" Shaggy asked.

"I think we've got a flat tire," Fred said.

He, Daphne, and Velma jumped out to have a look.

Scooby picked up the soccer ball and started spinning it on the tip of his tail. "Rey, Raggy, rook at ris," Scooby said.

"Not bad, Scoob," Shaggy said.

Fred opened the van's back doors.

"It's a flat, all right," he said. "We're right next to a construction site, so we must have hit a nail or something. Can you two climb out so we can get the spare?"

"Like, no problem, Fred-a-roony," Shaggy said. "Come on, Scoob. We can use the time to practice our penalty kicks."

"Not so fast," Velma said. "If we're going to get the flat changed in time to make the start of the game, everyone has to pitch in."

Fred took out the jack and lug wrench and placed them on the side of the road.

"I wonder what they're digging up," Daphne said, looking over the side of a deep construction pit.

Velma scanned the surroundings and nodded. "I think this is the planned expansion of the history museum," she said. "I read about it in the newspaper."

"Oh, that's right," Daphne said. "The old museum is just on the other side of this hill."

"Hey, Shaggy, give me a hand with the spare tire," Fred called. Shaggy walked over to the back of the van and helped lower the tire onto the ground.

"Now hold on to this while I get the jack set up," Fred said.

"Hey, Scooby, I'll bet you a slice of pizza you can't kick the soccer ball through the tire," Shaggy called.

"Rokay," Scooby replied.

Scooby put the ball down, lined up his shot, and gave the ball a strong kick. The ball sailed through the air and landed smack in the center of the tire.

"Roal!" Scooby cheered. "Rhere's my rizza?"

"Not so fast, Scoob," Shaggy said. "I bet you couldn't get the ball *through* the tire. It looks to me like it's stuck *inside* the tire, so it technically didn't go through. Looks like you owe me a slice of pizza."

"Roh way," Scooby said.

As Scooby and Shaggy argued about their bet, Shaggy took his hands off the tire. It rolled off the road and down a long dirt ramp used by the construction vehicles to get in and out of the work area.

"Ready for the spare, Shaggy," Fred called. Fred looked up and didn't see the tire anywhere. "Shaggy! Scooby! Where's the spare?"

Shaggy and Scooby stopped arguing and looked around.

"I don't know, Fred," Shaggy answered.

"There it is," Daphne said, pointing to the rolling tire.

"Looks like you two are going for a walk," Velma said.

When Shaggy and Scooby were halfway down the ramp, the rolling tire slammed into a large dirt wall. The ground trembled, and the wall suddenly collapsed.

"Zoinks!" Shaggy cried. "Earthquake!"

Chapter 2

The tremor knocked Shaggy and Scooby off their feet. They tumbled the rest of the way down the ramp.

"Hold on, fellas!" Fred called. "We're coming!"

Fred, Daphne, and Velma ran down and found Shaggy and Scooby sitting on the ground, covered with dirt.

"Are you two okay?" Daphne asked.

"Like, now I know what an avalanche feels like," Shaggy said.

"Reah, a rirty one," Scooby agreed. He

stood up and gave his body a good shake, sending a cloud of dust Shaggy's way.

The dust cleared from the far end of the construction area.

"Jinkies!" Velma gasped. "The whole wall is gone!"

A construction worker hopped out of a trailer parked next to the ramp. He wore a hard hat with a built-in light and an orange safety vest.

"What are you kids doing here?" the man asked. "This is a restricted construction site, not a park."

"Sorry, sir, but we lost our tire," Daphne said. "We got a flat up on the road and our spare tire rolled down in here."

"Boo-hoo for you," the man said.

"Is there a phone we can use to call a tow truck?" Fred asked.

"In the office," the man said, pointing to the trailer. "But make it snappy, and then get out of here."

The construction worker ran over to examine the opening in the wall. He turned on his hard hat light and carefully stepped into the opening.

"Is it just me, or do you notice anything strange about this construction site?" Velma asked.

Everyone looked around. They saw a bulldozer and steam shovel and piles of dirt covered with large blue tarps. A mess of shovels, pickaxes, and jackhammers were lying on the ground. A pile of hard hats sat just outside the office trailer.

"Looks like there's everything you'd need to dig a hole in the ground," observed Daphne.

"Ruh-uh," Scooby said. "Rall rou reed are

reese!" He held up his front paws and started digging a hole.

"Way to go, Scooby!" Shaggy cheered. "Like, all they really need here is a team of Scoobies to do the work."

"Or construction workers!" Fred said.

"Jeepers, you're right, Fred," Daphne said. "I wonder where everyone is."

"So do I," said a strange voice behind them. The gang looked over and saw a tall man in a dark suit. He had tufts of gray hair over each ear, bushy gray eyebrows, and wore a monocle over his right eye.

"I'm Q. Ford Umber," the man said. "Director of the Metropolitan Historical Society Museum."

"Nice to meet you, Mr. Umber," Daphne said. "I'm Daphne. And this is Fred, Velma, Shaggy, and Scooby-Doo."

"May I ask what you are doing here?" Mr. Umber said.

"Our van got a flat tire up there," Fred said. "When we went to change it, the spare got away from us and rolled down here. We were just coming down to get it when one of the dirt walls gave way."

"So that's what it was," Mr. Umber said. "I felt the tremor all the way in the museum on the other side of the hill. Do you know if anyone else is here?"

"We've only seen one person so far," Velma said. "And there he is."

The construction worker stepped out of the cave. As he walked toward the gang, he

appeared to be holding his right arm against his vest.

"Carl? Is that you?" Mr. Umber called.

"It's me, Mr. Umber," the worker called back.

"That's Carl Lumpkin, the construction foreman," Mr. Umber said. "Carl, what happened? Where is everyone?"

"One of the walls collapsed," Carl said.

"Opened up a cave that goes into the hill. Can't tell how far back it goes, but it looks really old. And I sent everyone home early today. We've been so far ahead of schedule, I figured they'd earned the half day." Carl shifted his right arm a bit.

"Is your arm all right?" Mr. Umber asked.

"Fine, fine," Carl replied. "Just, uh, tripped and banged it on a rock. I'm going to bandage it up right now." As Carl stepped away, he bumped into Scooby. A large brown rectangle fell out from under his vest.

"What's that?" Mr. Umber asked. He picked up the object before Carl could get his hands back on it. Mr. Umber looked at the brown rectangle and gently brushed away some dirt. "It's a book."

"And from the looks of it, a really old book," Velma said.

"Now, Carl, you know the rules about things you find," Mr. Umber said. "Remem-

ber, the museum is paying you to dig, not take things. Everything you find here belongs to the museum."

"Under that logic, Ford, everything found here belongs to me!" a deep voice bellowed.

Chapter 3

"What are you doing here, Morris?" Mr. Umber said.

"I thought I'd take a little stroll to check on the progress of the construction," the man replied. "Just making sure my money's being well spent."

"Excuse me, but this is a closed construction site," Carl Lumpkin said.

"Carl, this is Morris Mentchik," Mr. Umber said.

"Jinkies," Velma said. "Are you the same

Morris Mentchik whose name is going on the new building?"

"That's right," Morris said, smoothing the wrinkles out of his crisp white suit. "So what is it you found for me, Ford?"

"I found it," Carl interjected. "In that cave over there. It's a book."

"I was about to call Whitney Stavross and ask her to come take a look at it," Mr. Umber said as he took out his cell phone. "Whitney curates the museum's rare book collection." He had trouble dialing and holding on to the dirt-encrusted book at the same time. Finally, he gave up and handed the book to Mr. Mentchik.

Mr. Mentchik smiled. Carl scowled at Mr. Mentchik and then noticed Fred, Daphne, and Velma walking toward the cave.

"Hey, what are you kids doing?" Carl called.

"We just wanted to take one more look around for our tire," Fred said.

Carl looked over at Ford Umber. As he spoke on the phone, Ford waved to Carl, indicating it was okay.

"Fine, just put those things on," Carl said, pointing to a pile of orange hard hats. "You, too, Mr. Mentchik. This is a construction site, and safety rules apply to everyone."

Mr. Mentchik's eyes lit up. "Splendid!" he said. "I've always wanted to wear one of these."

Mr. Mentchik put the book on the ground and picked up one of the hats with a light on the front like Carl Lumpkin's. It didn't quite fit over Mr. Mentchik's large round head, so he carefully balanced it on top. The gang put on regular orange hard hats and started looking around.

"I remember seeing the tire bouncing

backward off the wall," Daphne said. "Maybe it rolled somewhere over there."

As Fred, Daphne, and Velma looked for the tire, Shaggy and Scooby wandered over to a steam shovel.

"Check it out, Scoob," Shaggy called. He climbed up into the operator's seat. "Just call me, like, Shovelin' Shaggy." He moved the controls back and forth, making steam shovel sounds.

"Shaggy, get down from there!" Daphne said.

"Like, sorry!" Shaggy said as he jumped down.

"We're supposed to be looking for the tire, which, if memory serves, had your soccer ball stuck inside it," Velma said.

"That's right!" Shaggy remembered. "Like, I totally forgot. Come on, Scoob, let's go find that soccer ball!"

Fred, Daphne, and Velma watched Shaggy and Scooby run off.

"We'd better go use the phone now," Fred said. "I don't think we're going to find our tire anywhere."

As the three of them walked toward the office trailer, they heard shouts coming from inside. The door burst open and Carl Lumpkin stomped down the stairs.

"What's wrong, Mr. Lumpkin?" Velma asked.

"What's wrong is that I do all the work

and never get the reward," he answered. "I'm the one who went into the cave, and I'm the one who found the book. I'm not saying I want to keep it or anything, but I deserve at least a little piece of the action."

The door opened again, and Ford Umber walked down the stairs behind Morris Mentchik. Morris was still holding the book.

"You're going to have to let it go eventually, Morris," Mr. Umber said. "So why not let me hold on to it until Whitney gets here?"

"Oh, no you don't, Umber," Morris said. "I'm not letting this book out of my hands until we know exactly what it's worth — I mean, what it's about."

"Whitney should be here any minute," Mr. Umber said.

"If not sooner," a woman's voice announced from behind them.

Chapter 4

"Whitney! You must have set a world record in getting over here," Mr. Umber said.

"When you called, I was in the middle of restoring an old manuscript," Whitney replied. "But I dropped everything and ran over here."

"Whitney Stavross is one of the foremost authorities on old books and rare manuscripts," Mr. Umber explained.

Whitney took the book from Mr. Mentchik and examined it from all sides and angles. Then she took a small paintbrush from her pocket and lightly dusted off one side of the book.

"Do you see anything?" Morris Mentchik asked. "What kind of book is it?"

"It's hard to tell with all this hardened earth on the cover," Whitney said. "But I think I can make out a few letters." Whitney held the book close to her eyes. "It says . . ."

Fred, Daphne, Velma, Mr. Umber, and Morris Mentchik leaned in to hear.

"S . . . p . . . e . . . l . . . and that's all I can make out," Whitney reported. "Where did you say you found this?"

"He didn't find it, I did!" Carl Lumpkin said. "In that cave."

"Cave?" Whitney said. Her eyes narrowed in deep thought, then her face lit up. "That's it!"

"What's it?" asked Morris Mentchik.

"This book and the cave," Whitney said. "I once came across an old manuscript that described this land as an ancient wizard's temple. The temple was built here right before the Revolutionary War by people who believed that Merlin and other wizards from English folklore were real people. They practiced all kinds of magic and sorcery. And this must be their book of spells."

"Book of spells? What kind of spells?" asked Morris Mentchik.

"I'm not sure, but they must have been very powerful," Whitney said.

"Surely you don't believe in wizards and spells, Whitney," Mr. Umber said.

"It doesn't matter what I believe, Ford," Whitney said. "These people did. What a wonderful addition to the museum this will be."

"Hold on there," Morris Mentchik said. "Let's not forget who's paying for all this work. Just hand the book over to me, Ms. Stavross."

"Why should you get it?" Carl Lumpkin interrupted. "I'm the one who did all the work finding it. Why can't I get a piece of the action?"

Whitney, Morris, and Carl began arguing over the book.

"Man, the silly things people argue about," Shaggy said. "I mean, like, it's just a book."

"I don't know, Shaggy," Velma said. "If Ms. Stavross is right, then it's more than just a

book. It's a book of very powerful magic spells."

"And it seems like three people have already fallen under its power," Mr. Umber said. "See here, you three. That's enough."

The arguing continued as Whitney, Morris, and Carl ignored Mr. Umber's pleas. Finally, Scooby put his paw in his mouth and gave a loud, piercing whistle.

The arguing stopped.

"Thank you, Scooby," Mr. Umber said. "Since I'm the only one who doesn't seem to have lost his senses over the book, I'm going to hold on to it for the time being. Whitney?"

Whitney slowly handed over the book.

"Now, let's put all this nonsense aside," Mr. Umber continued. "Carl, I want you to close the site until further notice. Whitney, I want you to research these wizards and find all references to a book of spells. This could be the biggest thing ever to happen to the museum."

"Can I borrow your cell phone, Ford?" Whitney asked. "There's someone I'd like to call over at the university, and my battery fizzled out on the way over here."

Ford Umber gave his cell phone to Whitney.

"Is there anything we can do to help, Mr. Umber?" asked Fred. "After all, we can't go anywhere until the tow truck gets here."

"Thanks, kids, but we've got it under control," Mr. Umber said. "You can hang out in the trailer until help arrives."

•

Chapter 5

Inside the construction trailer, the gang was becoming fidgety.

"Jeepers, inside an office trailer is just about the last place I'd like to be right now," Daphne said.

"I know what you mean, Daphne," Velma agreed. "I'd give anything to be able to explore that cave."

"Or take a look at that book," Fred said.

"Or have a pizza and a banana split," Shaggy added.

"Shaggy!" Daphne said. "How can you think about food at a time like this?"

"Like, it's easy, Daph," Shaggy said. "Let's show her, Scooby." Shaggy stood up and held his chin in his left hand. Scooby sat down and crossed his paws. Both of them stared off into space, smiling dreamily.

"Carl? Is that you?" they heard Mr. Umber yell. "Carl? Cut it out!"

Fred, Daphne, and Velma sprang into action. They leaped out of the trailer to find Ford Umber staring at an eerie light glowing from inside the cave. He clutched the book tightly.

"What is that?" Daphne asked.

"I thought it was Carl," Mr. Umber replied. "Now I'm not so sure." The four of them gazed into the cave, trying to see where the light was coming from.

Shaggy and Scooby walked over and peered over Daphne's shoulder.

"Like, what's up?" Shaggy asked.

Fred, Daphne, Velma, and Mr. Umber jumped and spun around.

"Shaggy, don't sneak up on us like that," Velma said.

"Sorry," Shaggy said. "We were just wondering where everybody went."

"There's something strange going on inside the cave," Fred said.

"Oh, it's just a wizard," Shaggy said.

"Wizard?" the others cried. Fred, Daphne, Velma, and Mr. Umber turned back to face

the cave. There in the entrance, his magic wand raised in the air, stood a wizard.

"Which one of you has stolen my book of spells?" the wizard asked in a ghostly voice.

"Ree did," Scooby said, pointing at Mr. Umber.

"Give me my book," the wizard demanded.

"I don't know who you are, but I'm certainly not giving you this book," Mr. Umber said.

"Then you shall pay the price," the wizard warned. He tapped his pointed hat with the tip of his wand. The wizard's hat started glowing. Then the wizard aimed his wand at Mr. Umber and uttered, "*Farfallin ent penne al dente con pomidorum!*"

"What did he say?" Daphne asked.

"Like, I don't know, but if there's one thing I do know, it's never argue with a wizard in a bad mood," Shaggy whispered to Scooby.

The wizard pointed his wand at Mr. Umber and the gang. A bright light shone in

31

everyone's eyes. Mr. Umber and the gang covered their eyes and turned away.

The wizard ran over to Mr. Umber and yanked the book from his hands. "I'll teach all of you to mess with a wizard!" he shouted. With his free hand, the wizard grabbed Daphne's wrist and ran back into the cave with her.

"We have to rescue Daphne!" Fred said.

"And the book of spells!" Mr. Umber cried. He ran into the cave and disappeared into the darkness.

The gang ran over to the mouth of the cave but quickly stopped.

"It's, like, pitch-black in there," Shaggy said.

"Daphne! Mr. Umber!" Fred shouted. "We're going to need some flashlights if we're going to find anything in there."

"I think I remember seeing some inside the trailer," Velma said.

"Great," Fred said. "You take Shaggy and Scooby to get them. I'll go in as far as I can to look for Daphne and make sure the wizard doesn't get away."

There was another flash of light from deep inside the cave.

"Jinkies!" Velma exclaimed. "What was that?"

Just then, a mouse ran by with something in its mouth.

"Hey, I've never seen a mouse that needs glasses before," Shaggy said.

Velma saw the mouse scurry away. "Those weren't glasses, Shaggy, that was a monocle," she said. "And the only person who was wearing one of those was Mr. Umber."

"Zoinks! That wizard turned Mr. Umber into a mouse!" Shaggy cried.

"Looks like we've got an even bigger mystery on our hands," Fred said.

Chapter 6

Velma, Shaggy, and Scooby ran to the trailer and returned with flashlights.

"Look what I found just inside the cave," Fred said. He showed the others a hard hat with a built-in light.

"The light looks like it was smashed," Velma said.

"Good thing we found these next to the trailer," Shaggy said, pointing to his head. Both he and Scooby wore hard hats with a built-in light. "After all, Scooby and I need to keep our hands free."

"Why is that?" asked Fred.

"In case we meet up with that wizard and need to do this," Shaggy said. He and Scooby raised their hands in the air and ran around in circles.

"Relp! A rizard!" Scooby barked.

"I'm sorry I asked," Fred said. "In addition to finding this clue, I also discovered that the cave branches off into a few different directions. We're going to have to split up. I'll take the tunnel on the left. Velma, you go in the middle. And Shaggy and Scooby, you two go to the right. As soon as you find something, come back here."

Fred turned on his flashlight and disappeared into the cave.

"Are you two ready?" Velma asked.

"Like, as ready as anyone who's about to walk into a creepy cave with a wizard that likes to change people into mice can be," Shaggy said. "Right, Scooby-Doo?"

Scooby nodded weakly. "Reah," he said.

"Then lights on, and let's go," Velma said. She flipped on her flashlight and walked into the cave. Shaggy and Scooby turned on their hat lights and followed her. A little ways inside the cave, a tunnel appeared on the right.

"Like, this is our turn, Scooby," Shaggy said. He and Scooby walked down the dark tunnel. The light from their hats cast eerie shadows along the cave's rocky walls.

"D-D-D-Daphne?" whispered Shaggy. "Daph? Oh, well, no sign of her here, Scoob. Let's go back the other way." Shaggy turned around. His hat light shone right at Scooby, projecting a silhouette against the cave wall.

"Look, Scooby," Shaggy said. "You're a shadow puppet."

Scooby turned his head and saw his shadow against the rocky wall. He moved his paws up and down.

"Ruess rhat rhis ris," he said. Scooby put his paws together and curled his tail up over them. The shadowy shape bounced along the wall.

"Like, it's a monkey in a tree eating a banana," Shaggy guessed.

"Right!" Scooby barked.

Scooby tried another shadow puppet, but the shape faded as the wall filled with light.

"Hey, who turned on the lights?" Shaggy asked.

"I did," a woman's voice said.

Shaggy and Scooby turned and saw a ghostly face with a light shining up from under its chin.

"Zoinks! It's a cave monster!" Shaggy cried.

"Relax, it's just me," Velma said, moving her flashlight. "What are you two up to?"

"We were, like, just taking a puppet break," Shaggy said. "How'd you find us, anyway?"

"It turns out that all of the tunnels in this cave crisscross one another," she said. "I've already bumped into Fred three times. And I found this."

Velma held up a small, torn piece of paper. "It's part of a pay stub from the museum," she said. "Do you know what this means?"

"That the wizard is a litterbug?" Shaggy asked.

He and Scooby giggled.

"No, Shaggy, it means we're getting closer to solving this mystery," Velma said. "I'm going to try to find Fred and show him this clue. You two can go back to the cave's entrance and keep an eye on things there."

Velma aimed her flashlight down the tunnel and went on her way. Shaggy and Scooby watched the light grow dimmer as Velma disappeared around a bend.

"Time for one more before we go, Scoob?" Shaggy asked.

"Reah." Scooby nodded.

This time, Scooby aimed his hat light at Shaggy. Shaggy put his hands together and made a shape. Scooby looked at the shape and started whimpering.

"What's the matter, Scooby?" asked Shaggy. "Afraid of a little bunny rabbit shadow puppet?"

"Ruh-uh," Scooby answered. "Ri'm afraid of a rizard radow ruppet."

Shaggy looked at his shadow puppet. Instead of a bunny rabbit, he saw a tall shadow with a pointed hat. Then he turned back to Scooby. The wizard was standing right behind him!

"Quick, Scooby, like we practiced!" Shaggy called.

"Relp! A rizard!" Scooby cried as he and Shaggy ran around in circles with their arms up in the air.

"Now, let's get out of here before he turns us into mice!"

Chapter 7

"We can't seem to shake him, Scoob," Shaggy panted. "It's like he knows where the tunnel's going before we even get there."

They ran around a bend in the tunnel and made a sharp left down a side passage. They pressed their bodies against the craggy walls and tried not to move.

"Turn off your light, Scooby," Shaggy said. They both turned off their hard hat lights and waited. A greenish glow filled the main part of the tunnel as the wizard slowly approached.

"Rikes!" Scooby whimpered.

Shaggy put his hand over Scooby's mouth.

"Shhhh!" he said. They watched the wizard pass right by their hideout and continue down the tunnel.

"Come on, Scooby," Shaggy said. "Maybe if we follow him he'll, like, lead us to Daphne." Shaggy and Scooby slid out of the side passage and tiptoed after the wizard. They followed the wizard down another narrow passage. The wizard stopped in front of a stone wall. A second later, he spun around.

"Zoinks! He's spotted us!" Shaggy cried.

"Don't move!" the wizard warned.

The wizard raised his magic wand and released a blinding flash of light. When Shaggy and Scooby opened their eyes, the wizard was gone.

"Hey, we're not mice!" Shaggy said.

"Re risappeared," Scooby noticed.

Shaggy and Scooby suddenly heard footsteps and saw a light at the far end of the passage. "Oh, no! He's coming after us for real this time!" Shaggy cried.

As the light approached them, Shaggy and Scooby slowly backed up against the stone wall.

"Man, it's a good thing I like cheese," Shaggy whispered to Scooby.

Shaggy and Scooby closed their eyes and pushed back against the wall. They felt something move, and then suddenly tumbled over backward.

"Shaggy! Scooby!"

It was Daphne's voice.

"Daph? Is that you?" Shaggy asked. He opened his eyes and looked up. There was Daphne, standing over him.

"Thank heavens you found me," she said. "I've been looking for the secret handle forever."

"Like, what secret handle?" asked Shaggy.

"The one that opens the secret door you

and Scooby found," Velma said. She and Fred stepped through the opening made by the stone door. The gang stood in a small, closet-sized space. On one side, the stone wall from the cave was opened like a door. On the other, a metal door was shut tight.

"Are you all right, Daphne?" Fred asked. "What happened?"

"I'm fine. I managed to get away from the wizard and hide inside one of the side passages," she said. "Once my eyes adjusted to the darkness, I saw a greenish glow in one of the tunnels. I followed the glow and saw the wizard open this door. But once I got inside, I realized I was trapped here. I couldn't get back into the cave, and this other door is locked."

"Where does the door go?" asked Velma.

"To the museum," Daphne said. "Just before Shaggy and Scooby dropped in, the wizard ran through in such a hurry he didn't see me. But I did manage to steal a quick glance through the door."

"It's a good thing he was in a hurry," Fred said. "Otherwise he might not have dropped this."

Fred picked a cell phone up off the floor.

"I think it's time for us to get out of this cave and make that wizard see the light," Velma said.

Fred nodded. "Velma's right," he said. "Gang, let's set a trap."

Chapter 8

"We need to lure the wizard out of the museum and back to the cave," Fred said.

"And the best way to do that is make him think we've found another book of spells," Velma continued.

"So let's go," Fred said. The gang found their way back through the cave to the construction site. Velma ran into the office trailer and came out with a set of keys.

"Here, Fred," she said, tossing the keys through the air.

"Thanks, Velma," Fred said, catching the keys. He climbed up into the steam shovel.

"Shaggy, Scooby, when I give the signal, you two start digging in that pile of dirt over there. After a few shovelfuls of dirt, pretend that you've found something valuable."

"Daphne, how about you and I take this rope and set up a trip line over there?" Velma said. "That way, we can get the wizard to fall into the scoop of the steam shovel."

"I'm sorry, everyone," Shaggy called. "But there are two things Scooby and I make it a point never to do. One is skipping a meal. The other is pretending to do construction work while trying to capture a wizard that turns people into mice."

"Don't worry, Shaggy," Daphne said. "We won't let the wizard turn you and Scooby into mice."

"Well, he's got a whole book of spells," Shaggy said. "Who said it has to be mice? Maybe it'll be, like, a cow."

"Or a rig," Scooby said.

"Or a duck-billed platypus," Shaggy said.

"Or a rippopotamus," Scooby said.

"Or a —"

"We get the picture, fellas," Velma interrupted. "So what will it take to get you to help us? Maybe a Scooby Snack?"

Scooby's ears perked up.

"Raybe," he said.

"How about several Scooby Snacks?" Daphne asked.

"Roh, boy!" Scooby barked. "Rou bet!"

Daphne and Velma each tossed some snacks to Scooby. In the

blink of an eye, he gobbled them down. "Ret's ret ro work!"

Fred fired up the steam shovel and lowered the scoop. Daphne and Velma set the trip line along the ground and hid. Shaggy and Scooby picked up their shovels and started digging.

"Man, how is it you always end up getting the snacks and I always end up doing the work?" Shaggy moaned.

Shaggy buried his shovel into the dirt pile. "Hey!" he exclaimed. "I hit something. There's something in here, Scooby."

"Rhat ris rit?" Scooby asked.

"Like, I don't know," Shaggy said loudly. "Maybe it's another one of those secret books of magic spells."

Shaggy dug farther into the dirt pile. He lay down his shovel and reached into the pile.

"Hey, Scoob, look at this!" he cried. Shaggy stood up, holding the spare tire with the soccer ball inside. "We found it!"

Shaggy tossed the ball up into the air and bounced it a couple of times on his knees. As he and Scooby passed the ball back and forth, another figure joined them.

"Where is the other book?" shouted the wizard.

"Like, heads up, Scoob!" Shaggy called. Shaggy bounced the soccer ball off his head to Scooby, who headed it over to the wizard. The ball knocked the magic wand out of the wizard's hand and then rolled away.

"Ruh-roh," Scooby said. "Rorry."

The wizard raised his hands and cast a spell at Scooby.

"*Saladum ceasarim mit croutonin!*" chanted the wizard.

Shaggy noticed Daphne motioning toward the steam shovel.

"Come on, Scooby," Shaggy said as he ran around the big pile of earth.

Scooby ran the other way around the dirt

pile and they collided on the other side. Shaggy staggered backward and fell over the trip line. He tumbled into the steam shovel scoop, and Fred raised the scoop into the sky.

"Like, you got the wrong guy!" Shaggy called down. "The wizard's still after Scooby!"

The wizard chased Scooby around the construction site and into the cave.

"I've got you now!" the wizard cried.

A moment later, the wizard ran out. Scooby followed him. The wizard, looking over his shoulder at Scooby, didn't see Fred quickly lower the scoop. In an instant, Shaggy jumped out and the wizard tumbled in. Fred raised the scoop. The wizard was caught!

Chapter 9

"**G**et me out of here!" the wizard shouted from the scoop.

"Not until you tell us what you did to Mr. Umber," Daphne called back.

"He didn't do anything to me," Mr. Umber said as he staggered out of the cave. He had a big bump on his forehead. "When I went into the cave after him, I must have banged my head on a rock. I think I've been unconscious the whole time."

"You mean, like, the wizard didn't turn you into a mouse?" Shaggy asked.

"A what?" Mr. Umber said.

"Never mind, Mr. Umber," Fred said. "Now, would you like to see who's really behind this mystery?"

Mr. Umber nodded slowly. Fred lowered the steam shovel scoop far enough so that Mr. Umber could reach up and pull off the wizard's hat and mask.

"Whitney Stavross!" Mr. Umber exclaimed. "*You* were the wizard? You stole the book of spells? I don't understand."

"We do," Velma said. "Though at first we weren't completely sure. The first clue we found was one of those hard hats with the lights on them. The wizard put his own hat over the hard hat to make it seem like it was glowing."

"Only three people at the site were wearing that kind of hard hat," Daphne said. "Ms. Stavross, Carl Lumpkin, and Morris Mentchik. And if you'll recall, Mr. Umber, all three of them argued over who should get the book."

"Yes, I remember that," Mr. Umber said.

"The next clue we found didn't exactly tell us who it was," Fred said. "But it did tell us who it wasn't."

He showed Mr. Umber the torn pay stub they found.

"That's a museum pay stub," Mr. Umber confirmed.

"And of the three suspects, the only one not paid by the museum was Morris Mentchik," Velma explained.

A loud chuckle caught everyone's attention.

"I'm rich — I mean, that's rich." Morris Mentchik laughed. "Imagine me, working for the museum."

"Where have you been, Mr. Mentchik?" Daphne asked.

"Consulting with my attorneys," he said. "Turns out Ford here was right. Anything found on the site belongs to the museum, not me."

"So that left Carl Lumpkin and Ms. Stavross," Velma said.

"Then Shaggy and Scooby found Daphne and the secret passage to the museum," Fred said. "We found a cell phone there, and that's when all the pieces fell into place."

Mr. Umber still looked puzzled.

"Ms. Stavross used the secret passage to

get here so unbelievably fast after you called her," Daphne explained. "She knew about the cave from the old manuscripts she told us about."

"But how did she get through the cave?" asked Mr. Umber. "It's as dark as night in there, and I don't remember her having a flashlight."

"I'll show you," Fred said. "Shaggy, Scooby, keep an eye on Ms. Stavross."

Mr. Umber and Morris Mentchik followed Fred, Daphne, and Velma just inside the cave. After their eyes got used to the darkness, Fred turned on Mr. Umber's cell phone. The tiny screen and keypad glowed with a greenish light.

"Ms. Stavross used her cell phone to light the way," Velma said. "But her battery died, so she asked to borrow your phone, Mr. Umber. That way she could get around the cave without drawing attention to herself. She used a regular flashlight as part of her magic wand."

They returned to the steam shovel and looked up at Whitney Stavross.

"Why did you do it, Whitney?" asked Mr. Umber.

"Because I wanted to do more with my life than take care of old books," she said. "I wanted to learn the secrets of the wizards of old so I could use their magic to gain wealth and power! And I would have gotten away with it if it weren't for those kids and their meddlesome mutt."

"So where's the book of spells, Whitney?" Mr. Umber asked.

Whitney reached beneath her wizard's robe and produced the dirt-encrusted volume. "You and your dog want it so badly?" she asked. "Fetch!"

She tossed the book through the air and it landed outside the cave with a thud. The force of the impact knocked all of the hardened dirt from the book. Mr. Umber picked up the book and started laughing.

"What's so funny?" Whitney Stavross shouted.

Mr. Umber walked over and held up the book for Whitney to see. Her eyes widened in horror as she read the title.

"What is it, Mr. Umber?" Fred asked.

"It's not a book of spells," Mr. Umber said.

"It's — it's a book of spelling," said Whitney Stavross. "All this for a filthy old ABC's book? I can't believe it!"

Everyone but Whitney Stavross burst into laughter.

"Thanks so much, kids, and you, too, Scooby," Mr. Umber said. "You really scored one for the museum!"

"Scooby-Dooby-Doo!" cheered Scooby as the soccer ball spun on his tail.

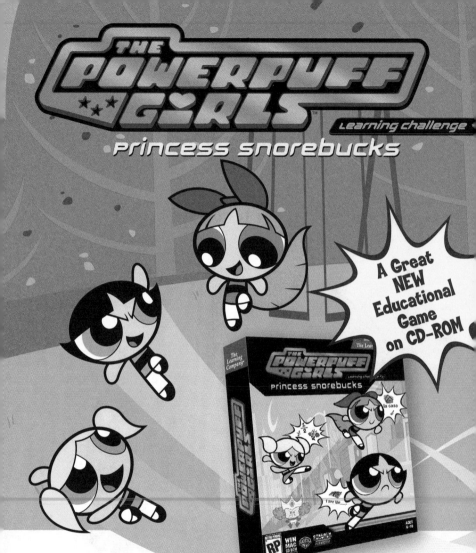

THE POWERPUFF GIRLS
Learning challenge
princess snorebucks

A Great NEW Educational Game on CD-ROM

Coming September 2003

Look for Learning Challenge #1, *Mojo Jojo's Clone Zone*. Available Now!

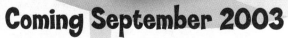
The Learning Compa